Yosl Rakover Talks to God

Zvi Kolitz

Yosl Rakover
Talks to God

Translated by Carol Brown Janeway

From the edition established by Paul Badde

*Afterwords by Emmanuel Lévinas
and Leon Wieseltier*

PANTHEON BOOKS

NEW YORK

All rights reserved under International and Pan-American
Copyright Conventions. Published in the United States by
Pantheon Books, a division of Random House, Inc., New York,
and simultaneously in Canada by Random House of Canada
Limited, Toronto. Originally published in Germany as
Jossel Rakovers Wendung zu Gott by Verlag Volk und
Welt GmbH, Berlin, in 1996. Copyright © 1996
by Verlag Volk und Welt GmbH, Berlin.
Pantheon Books and colophon are registered
trademarks of Random House, Inc.

The afterword by Emmanuel Lévinas was originally published
in *Yossel Rakover s'adresse à Dieu* by Calmann-Lévy,
Paris, in 1963. Copyright © 1963 by Albin Michel.

Kolitz, Zvi, 1913–
[Yosl Rakovers vendung tsu Got. English]
Yosl Rakover talks to God / Zvi Kolitz ; translated
by Carol Brown Janeway; from the edition
established by Paul Badde.
p.   cm.
ISBN 0-375-40451-1
1. Holocaust, Jewish (1939–1945)—Poland—Warsaw—Fiction.
2. Kolitz, Zvi, 1913– . 3. Holocaust (Jewish theology)
I. Janeway, Carol Brown.   II. Title.
PJ5129.K549Y6713 1999
892.4'36—dc21   99-20734   CIP
Random House Web Address: www.randomhouse.com

Book design by Johanna Roebas

Printed in the United States of America

First Edition

2 4 6 8 9 7 5 3 1

I believe in the sun, even when it doesn't shine.
I believe in love, even when I don't feel it.
I believe in God, even when He is silent.

—Inscription on the wall of a cellar
   in Cologne where some Jews remained
   hidden for the entire duration of the war

Contents

YOSL RAKOVER TALKS TO GOD

In one of the ruins of the Warsaw Ghetto, preserved in a little bottle and concealed amongst heaps of charred stone and human bones, the following testament was found, written in the last hours of the ghetto by a Jew named Yosl Rakover.

Warsaw, 28 April 1943

I, Yosl, son of David Rakover of Tarnopol, a follower of the Rabbi of Ger and descendant of the righteous, learned, and holy ones of the families Rakover and Maysels, am writing these lines as the houses of the Warsaw Ghetto are in flames, and the house I am in is one of the last that has not yet caught fire. For several hours now we have been under raging artillery fire and all around me walls are exploding and shattering in the hail of shells. It will not be long before this house I'm in, like almost all the houses in the ghetto, will become the grave of its inhabitants and defenders.

Fiery red bolts of sunlight piercing through the little half-walled-up window in my room, out of which we've been shooting at the enemy day and night, tell me that it must be almost evening, just before sundown. The sun probably has no idea how little I regret that I shall never see it again.

A strange thing has happened to us: all our ideas and feelings have changed. Death, quick death that comes in an instant, is to us a deliverer, a liberator who breaks our chains. The animals of the forest seem so dear and precious to me that it pains my heart to hear the criminals who are now masters of Europe likened to them. It is not true that there is something of the animal in Hitler. He is—I am utterly convinced of it—a typical child of modern man. Mankind has borne him and raised him and he is the direct, unfeigned expression of mankind's innermost, deepest-hidden urges.

In a forest where I was hiding, I met a dog one night, a sick, starving, crazed dog, his tail between his legs. Immediately we felt our common situation, for no dog's situation is a whit better than our own. He rubbed up against me, buried his head in my lap, and licked my hands. I don't know if I have ever wept the way I wept that night; I wrapped myself around his neck and cried like a child. If I stress the fact that I envied the animals then, no one should be surprised. But what I felt back then was more than envy; it was shame. I was ashamed before the dog, for being not a dog but a man. That is how it is, and such is the spiritual condition we have reached: life is a calamity—death, a liberator—man, a plague—beast, an ideal—day, an abomination—night, a comfort.

Millions of people in the great, wide world, in love with the day, the sun, and the light, neither know nor have the slightest intimation of the darkness and calamity the sun brings us. The criminals have made of it an instrument in their hands; they have used the sun as a searchlight to reveal the footprints of the fugitives trying to escape them. When I hid myself in the forests with my wife and my children—there were six of them then—it was the night, only the night, that concealed us in her heart. The day delivered us to our pursuers, who were hunting our souls. How can I ever forget the day of that German firestorm that raged over thousands of refugees on the road from Grodno to Warsaw?

Their planes rose in the early dawn with the sun, and all day long they slaughtered us unceasingly. In this massacre that came down from the skies my wife died with our youngest child, seven months old, in her arms, and two of my surviving five children vanished that same day without a trace. David and Jehuda were their names, the one was four years old, the other six.

When the sun went down the handful of survivors moved on again toward Warsaw. But I combed through the woods and fields with my three remaining children, searching for the other two on the slaughterground. "David!—Jehuda!"—all night long our cries slashed like knives through the deadly silence that surrounded us, and all that answered us from the woods was an echo, helpless, heartrending, suffering as we suffered, a distant voice of lamentation. I never saw the two boys again, and I was told in a dream not to worry over them any more: they were in the hands of the Lord of Heaven and Earth. My other three children died in the Warsaw Ghetto within a year.

Rachel, my little daughter, ten years old, had heard that there were scraps of bread to be found in the city garbage cans on the other side of the walls of the ghetto. The ghetto was starving, and the starving lay like rags in the streets. People were prepared to die any death, but not death by starvation. This is probably because in a time when systematic persecution gradually destroys every other human need, the will to eat is the last one that endures, even in the presence of a longing for death. I was told of a Jew, half-starved, who said to someone, "Ah, how happy I would be to die if one last time I could sit down to a meal like a *mentsh*!"

Rachel had said nothing to me about her plan to steal out of the ghetto—a crime that carried the death penalty. She went off on her dangerous journey with a friend, another girl of the same age. In the dark of night she left home and at dawn she was discovered with her little friend outside the gates of the ghetto. The Nazi sentries and dozens of their Polish helpers immediately went in pursuit of the Jewish children who had dared to hunt in the garbage for a lump of bread so as not to die of hunger. People who had experienced this human hunt at first hand could not believe what they were seeing. Even for the ghetto this was new. You might have thought that dangerous escaped criminals were being chased as this terrifying pack ran amok after the two half-starved ten-year-old children. They couldn't keep up this race for long before one of them, my daughter, having expended the last of her strength, collapsed on the ground in exhaustion. The Nazis drove holes through her skull. The other girl escaped their clutches, but she died two weeks later. She had lost her mind.

Jacob, our fifth child, a boy of thirteen, died of tuberculosis on the day of his bar mitzvah. His death was a release for him. The last child, my daughter Eva, lost her life at the age of fifteen in a "roundup of children" that began at sunrise on the final Rosh Hashanah and lasted till sundown.

On that first day of the New Year, hundreds of Jewish families lost their children before evening came.

Now my hour has come, and like Job I can say of myself—naked shall I return unto the earth, naked as the day I was born. My years are forty-three, and when I look back on the years that have gone by, I can say with certainty—insofar as any man may be certain of himself—that I have lived an honorable life. My heart has been filled with the love of God. I have been blessed with success, but the success never went to my head. My portion was ample. But though it was mine, I treated it not as mine: following the counsel of my rabbi, I considered my possessions to have no possessor. Should they lure someone to take some part of them, this should not be counted as theft, but as though that person had taken unclaimed goods. My house stood open for all who were needy, and I was happy when I was given the opportunity to perform a good deed for others. I served God with devotion, and my only petition of Him was that He allow me to serve Him "with all my heart and with all my soul and with all my strength."

I cannot say, after all I have lived through, that my relation to God is unchanged. But with absolute certainty I can say that my faith in Him has not altered by a hairsbreadth. In earlier times, when my life was good, my relation to Him was as if to one who gave me gifts without end, and to whom I was therefore always somewhat in debt. Now my relation to Him is as to one who is also in my debt—greatly in my debt. And because I feel that He too is in my debt, I consider that I have the right to *admonish* Him. I do not say, like Job, that God should lay His finger on my sins so that I may know how I have earned this. For greater and better men than I are convinced that it is no longer a question of punishment for sins and transgressions. On the contrary, something unique is happening in the world: *hastoras ponim*—God has hidden His face.

God has hidden His face from the world and delivered mankind over to its own savage urges and instincts. This is why I believe that when the forces of evil dominate the world, it is, alas, completely natural that the first victims will be those who represent the holy and the pure. To each of us as individuals, perhaps this brings no comfort. Yet as the destiny of our people is determined not by worldly but by otherworldly laws, not material and physical but spiritual and godly, so must the true believer see in these events a part of God's great leveling of the scales, in which even human tragedies weigh little. But this does not mean that the devout among my people must simply approve what is ordained and say, "The Lord is just and His decrees are just." To say that we have earned the blows we have received is to slander ourselves. It is a defamation of the *Shem Hameforash*, a profanation of His Holy Name —a desecration of the name "Jew," a desecration of the name "God." It is one and the same. God is blasphemed when we blaspheme ourselves.

In such a circumstance I have, naturally, no expectation of a miracle and do not beg of Him, my

Lord, that He should take pity on me. Let Him veil His face in indifference to me as He has veiled it to millions of others of His people. I am no exception to the rule. I expect no preference. I will no longer try to save myself, and I will not flee again from here. I will lighten the work of the fire and pour gasoline over my clothes. I still have three bottles of gasoline in reserve, after pouring several dozen over the heads of the murderers.

That was a great moment in my life, and I was convulsed with laughter. I could never have imagined that the death of people, even enemies— even enemies such as these—could fill me with such joy. Foolish humanists may say what they will, revenge and the longing for retribution have always fueled the resistance of the oppressed to the very last, and will always do so. Nothing else brings such solace to their souls. Until now I had never really understood the passage in the Talmud that says, "Vengeance is holy, for it is mentioned between two names of God, as it is written: *A God of vengeance is the Lord!*" Now I understand it. Now I feel it, and now I know why my heart rejoices when I remember how for thousands of years we have called upon our God: "God of Vengeance!" *El Nekamot Adonoi.*

And now, when I am in a position to view life and the world from this clearest of perspectives, such as is rarely granted a man before death, I realize that there is this exclusive and characteristic difference between our God and the God in whom the peoples of Europe believe: while our God is the God of vengeance and our Torah threatens death for the smallest of transgressions, it is also told in the Talmud how in ancient times, when the Sanhedrin was our people's highest court—when we were still a free people in our own land—a single death sentence from the High Council in seventy years was enough to make people call "You murderers" after the judges. The God of the other peoples, however, whom they call "the God of Love," has offered to love every creature created in His image, and yet they have been murdering us without pity in His name day in, day out, for almost two thousand years.

Yes, I speak of vengeance. Only rarely have we seen true vengeance, but when we have experienced it, it was so comforting, and so sweet, such deep solace and intense happiness, that to me it was as if a new life had opened up. A tank suddenly broke through into our alley and was bombarded from every fortified house around it with bottles of burning gasoline. But not one of them found its mark the way it was supposed to. The tank continued to advance undamaged. I waited with my friends until the tank was rumbling past, literally right under our noses, then we all attacked it at the same moment through the half-walled-up windows. The tank immediately burst into flames and six burning Nazis leapt out of it. Yes, they burned! They burned like the Jews whom they burned, but they screamed more than the Jews. The Jews do not scream. They embrace death as their deliverer. The Warsaw Ghetto is dying in battle, it is going down in gunfire, in fighting, and in flames—but there is no screaming.

I still have three bottles of gasoline left, and they are as precious to me as wine to a drinker. When not long from now I empty one of them over me, I will put the sheets of paper on which I am writing these lines into the empty bottle and hide it here between the bricks in the wall beneath the window. If anyone should ever find them and read them, he will perhaps understand the feeling of a Jew—one of millions—who died abandoned by God, in Whom he so deeply believes. I will explode the two other bottles over the heads of the thugs when my last moment is come.

We were twelve people in this room when the uprising began, and we have fought the enemy for nine days. All of my eleven comrades have fallen. They died silently. Even the little boy—God only knows where he came from, he was all of five years old—now lies dead beside me. His beautiful face is smiling, the way children smile when they are peacefully dreaming. Even this little boy died as calmly as his older comrades. It was early this morning. Most of us were already no longer alive. The boy clambered up the pile of corpses to catch a glimpse through the window slit of the world outside. He stood beside me that way for several minutes. Then he suddenly fell backwards, rolled down over the bodies of the dead, and lay there like a stone. A drop of blood appeared between two locks of black hair on his small, pale forehead. A bullet in the head.

Our house is one of the last bastions of the ghetto. Until early yesterday morning, when the enemy opened concentrated fire on this building with the first light of dawn, everyone here was still alive. Five had been wounded, but they kept fighting. Yesterday and today, one after the other, they all fell. One after the other, one on top of the other, each standing guard for the other and shooting until they themselves were shot.

Apart from the three bottles of gasoline, I have no more ammunition. There is still heavy gunfire coming from the three floors above me, but it seems they cannot send me help any more. The staircase appears to have been destroyed by shells, and I think the whole house may soon collapse. I am lying on the floor as I write these lines. All around me, my dead friends. I look into their faces and it is as if irony had washed over them, peaceful and gently mocking. As if they wanted to say: "Have a little patience, you foolish man, another minute or two and everything will become clear to you, too." The same expression hovers about the lips of the child, who is stretched out as if asleep by my right hand. His little mouth is smiling, as if he were laughing to himself. And to me—still breathing and feeling and thinking like a living creature made of flesh and blood—to me it seems as if he's laughing at me. As if he sees through me. He's laughing at me, with the quiet, meaningful laugh of one who knows much yet must endure talking with people who know nothing but think they know it all. He knows it all now, this little boy, it's all clear to him now. He even knows why he was born if he had to die so soon, and why he had to die now—and this in just five years. And even if he doesn't know why, he knows that knowing why or not knowing why is utterly irrelevant and unimportant in the light of the revelation of God's majesty in that better world where he is now—perhaps in the arms of his murdered parents, to whom he has found his way back.

In an hour or two I shall know it, too. And if the fire does not consume my face, perhaps there will be a similar smile on it when I am dead. But I am still alive. And before I die I want to speak to my God once more as a living man, an ordinary living man who had the great but terrible honor of being a Jew.

I am proud to be a Jew—not despite of the world's relation to us, but precisely because of it. I would be ashamed to belong to the peoples who have borne and raised the criminals responsible for the deeds that have been perpetrated against us.

I am proud of my Jewishness. Because being a Jew is an art. Being a Jew is hard. There is no art in being an Englishman, an American, or a Frenchman. It is perhaps easier and more comfortable to be one of them, but it is not more honorable. Yes, it is an honor to be a Jew.

I believe that to be a Jew is to be a fighter, an eternal swimmer against the roiling, evil current of humanity. The Jew is a hero, a martyr, a saint. You, our enemies, say that we are bad? I believe we are better than you, finer. But even if we were worse— I'd like to have seen how you would have looked in our place.

I am happy to belong to the unhappiest of all peoples in the world, whose Torah embodies the highest law and the most beautiful morality. Now this Torah is the more sanctified and immortalized by the manner of its rape and violation by the enemies of God.

Being a Jew is an inborn virtue, I believe. One is born a Jew as one is born an artist. One cannot free oneself of being a Jew. That is God's mark upon us, which sets us apart as His chosen people. Those who do not understand this will never grasp the higher meaning of our martyrdom. "There is nothing more whole than a broken heart," a great rabbi once said; and there is also no people more chosen than a permanently maligned one. If I were unable to believe that God had marked us for His chosen people, I would still believe that we were chosen to be so by our sufferings.

I believe in the God of Israel, even when He

has done everything to make me cease to believe in Him. I believe in His laws even when I cannot justify His deeds. My relationship to Him is no longer that of a servant to his master, but of a student to his rabbi. I bow my head before His greatness, but I will not kiss the rod with which He chastises me. I love Him. But I love His Torah more. Even if I were disappointed in Him, I would still cherish His Torah. God commands religion, but His Torah commands a way of life—and the more we die for this way of life, the more immortal it is!

And so, my God, before I die, freed from all fear, beyond terror, in a state of absolute inner peace and trust, I will allow myself to call You to account one last time in my life.

You say that we have sinned? We surely have! And for this shall we be punished? This, too, I understand. But I want You to tell me if there is any sin in the world that deserves the punishment we have received.

You say that You will yet take revenge on our enemies? I am convinced that you will revenge yourself on them without mercy, of this I have no doubt either. But I want You to tell me if there is any punishment in the world sufficient to atone for the crimes that have been perpetrated against us.

Perhaps You are saying that it is not a question of sin and punishment now, but that it is always so when You veil Your face and leave mankind to its inner drives? But then, God, I wish to ask You, and this question burns in me like a consuming fire: What more, O tell us, what more must happen before You reveal Your face to the world again?

I wish to speak to You clearly and frankly, to say that now, more than at any previous stage on our endless road of suffering—we, the tormented, the reviled, the suffocated, the buried alive and burned alive, we, the humiliated, the mocked, the ridiculed, the slaughtered in our millions—now more than ever do we have the right to know: Where are the limits of Your patience?

And I wish to say something more to You: You should not pull the rope too tight, because it might, heaven forbid, yet snap. The temptation into which You have led us is so grievous, so unbearably grievous, that You should, You must, forgive those of Your people who in their misery and anger have turned away from You.

Forgive those who have turned away from You in their misery, but also those of Your people who have turned away from You for their own comfort. You have made our life such an unending and unbearable struggle that the weaklings among us were compelled to try to elude it. To flee wherever they saw a line of escape. Do not strike them down for this! Weaklings are not to be struck down, weaklings call forth mercy. Lord, have mercy on them—more than on us!

Forgive also those who have taken Your name in vain, who have followed other gods, who have become indifferent to You. You have tested them so severely that they no longer believe You are their father, that they have any father at all.

I am saying all this to You in plain words because I believe in You, because I believe in You more than ever before, because I know now that You are my God. For You are not, You cannot be the God of those whose deeds are the most horrific proof of their militant godlessness.

For if You are not my God—whose God are You? The God of the murderers?

If those who hate me, who murder me, are so dark, so evil, who, then, am I if not one who embodies some spark of Your light and Your goodness?

I cannot praise You for the deeds You tolerate. But I bless and praise Your very existence, Your terrible majesty. How mighty it must be if even what is taking place now makes no impression on You!

But because You are so great and I so small, I beg You—I warn You—for Your name's sake: Stop crowning Your greatness by veiling Your face from the scourging of the wretched!

Nor do I beg You to scourge the guilty. It is part of the terrible logic of the inexorable decrees that they will come face to face with themselves at the end, because in our death dies the conscience of the world, because a world has been murdered in the murder of Israel.

The world will consume itself in its own evil, it will drown in its own blood.

The murderers have already pronounced judgment on themselves, and they will not escape it. But You, I beg You, pronounce Your guilty verdict, a doubly harsh verdict, on those who witness murder and remain silent!

On those who condemn murder with their lips while they rejoice over it in their hearts.

On those who say in their wicked hearts: Yes, it is true that the tyrant is evil, but he is also doing a job for which we will always be grateful to Him.

It is written in Your Torah that the thief must be punished more severely than the robber, although the thief does not attack his victim and threaten him, life and limb, but merely tries to deprive him of his property by stealth.

The robber attacks his victim in the broad light of day. He has as little fear of men as he does of God.

The thief, on the other hand, fears men, but not God. This is why his punishment should be more severe than the punishment of the robber.

So I do not mind if You treat the murderers as robbers, because their behavior to You and to us is the same. They make no secret of their murders and of their hatred of You and us.

Those, however, who remain silent in the face of murder, those who do not fear You but fear what people will say (Idiots! They don't know that people will say nothing!), those who express their sympathy for the drowning man but refuse to save him, those—oh, those, I swear to You, my God, are the ones You should punish like the thief!

Death cannot wait any longer, and I must finish what I am writing. The gunfire from the floors above me is diminishing by the minute. The last defenders of our fortress are falling, and with them Warsaw, the great, the beautiful, the God-fearing Jewish Warsaw, falls and dies. The sun is going down now, and thanks be to God I shall never see it again. The glow of the inferno flickers through the window, and the little piece of sky I can see is flooded in flaming red like a waterfall of blood. Another hour at most and I will be with my family, and with the millions of the dead among my people in that better world where there is no more doubt and God's hand rules supreme.

I die at peace, but not pacified, conquered and beaten but not enslaved, bitter but not disappointed, a believer but not a supplicant, a lover of God but not His blind Amen-sayer.

I have followed Him, even when He pushed me away. I have obeyed His commandments, even when He scourged me for it. I have loved Him, I have been in love with Him and remained so, even when He made me lower than the dust, tormented me to death, abandoned me to shame and mockery.

My rabbi used to tell me, again and again, the story of a Jew who escaped the Spanish Inquisition with his wife and child and made his way in a small boat across the stormy sea to a stony island. A flash of lightning exploded and killed his wife. A whirl-wind arose and hurled his child into the sea. Alone, wretched, discarded like a stone, naked and bare-foot, lashed by the storm, terrified by thunder and lightning, his hair disheveled and his hands raised to God, the Jew made his way up onto the rocky desert island and turned thus to God:

"God of Israel," he said, "I have fled to this place so that I may serve You in peace, to follow Your commandments and glorify Your name. You, however, are doing everything to make me cease believing in You. But if You think that You will suc-ceed with these trials in deflecting me from the true path, then I cry to You, my God and the God of my parents, that none of it will help You. You may in-sult me, You may chastise me, You may take from me the dearest and the best that I have in the world, You may torture me to death—I will always believe in You. I will love You always and forever—even despite You."

Here, then, are my last words to You, my angry God: None of this will avail You in the least! You have done everything to make me lose my faith in You, to make me cease to believe in You. But I die exactly as I have lived, an unshakeable believer in You.

Praised be forever the God of the dead, the God of vengeance, of truth and judgment, who will soon unveil His face to the world again and shake its foundations with His almighty voice.

"*Sh'ma Yisroel!* Hear, Israel! The Lord is our God, the Lord is one. Into Your hands, O Lord, I commend my soul."

Zvi Kolitz

by Paul Badde

"Yes?"—The connection is a little crackly.
—"Mr. Kolitz?"—"Yes."—"Zvi Kolitz?"—"Yes."
—"Are you the man who wrote *Yosl Rakover*?"—
"Yes." Have I turned dumb? I hear a faint cough
on the other end of the line, on the other side of the
Atlantic. "Who are you?" he asks. I tell him. Of
course I can come and visit him, any time. I falter
again.

This happened years ago. But as long as I
have my wits about me, I will never forget how I got
to know Zvi Kolitz.

Everything I knew about him until then had
made me suppose that he was long dead. I had not
been able to find his name in any archive or register.
"Give it up," a friend advised. "And what's the
point of looking for the author? This text tran-

scends the author." Is such a thing possible? In any case, it was impossible to forget him, impossible not to search for traces of him. He wouldn't let go of me.

I had asked an acquaintance in New York, where as I knew he must have lived in the fifties, if she could at least locate his grave in Manhattan or Brooklyn.

"Impossible!" she replied. "And who on earth was Zvi Kolitz?" But then, the very next day, she sent me his complete address, from the telephone book, where she'd found it between a David Kolitz on Sixty-fifth Street and a Nicholas Kolitz on Eighty-seventh Street: on Central Park South.

Seven days later we were sitting facing each other in his apartment. I was struck first by his Roman nose and the line of his mouth, then by his eyes, then his ramrod-straight bearing as soon as he stood up and moved. I realized only much later how fine-boned he is. Faint traces of the cacophony of horns on Columbus Circle drifted up from below. Zvi Kolitz was almost submerged in the brocade-covered armchair from which he inspected me with alert eyes, a painting of a snow-covered town in Eastern Europe above his head. I often met and talked with him after that, but the beginning was the key to everything that came afterwards. Suddenly the story had become a book from which you look up to find that you are in the midst of what you have just been reading, there on the pages you were just leafing through, your finger stuck in the book to mark your place.

I had never heard their names until a friend made them known to me a few months earlier, in the fall of 1992, a few days after my mother's death: Zvi Kolitz and Yosl Rakover, creator and creation of a lost—and found—masterpiece that could be squeezed onto two tightly written pages and kept disappearing again.

"Just read it! Here's someone who still knows something about faith!" he said as he pulled some carelessly photocopied pages out of his briefcase and put them on my desk. Even the typeface was of another era, the title more so: *Yosl Rakover Talks to God*. I read the pages at one sitting, as soon as I was alone again. Then I trimmed them neatly, enlarged them, and made a fresh, more presentable set of copies. Next day I showed the story to my sons and daughters. Then I sent it on to my brothers and friends, then to acquaintances, colleagues, and relatives. I couldn't just keep it to myself.

Few texts can have brought so many people

to tears. Why had I never found it in an anthology? It is a piece of poetry that burns away the very framework of literature like a jet of fire, with a Shakespearean intensity, and the gravity and presence of Job himself. Yet it was neither a poet nor a prophet who wrote this soliloquy, but a young journalist and secret agent, Zvi Kolitz. He wasn't even thirty at the time. I examine him surreptitiously as he talks about his life.

My friend had stumbled across mention of the piece in an essay written by the philosopher Emmanuel Lévinas in the late fifties, when *Yosl Rakover* was discovered in France, in the days of Jean-Paul Sartre and Albert Camus. "What is the meaning of the suffering of innocents?" Lévinas asked.

Does it not prove a world without God, an earth on which man is the only measure of good and evil? The simplest and most common reaction would be to decide for atheism. This would also be the reasonable reaction of all those whose idea of God until that point was of some kindergarten deity who distributed prizes, applied penalties, or forgave faults and in His goodness treated men as eternal children. But . . . with

what kind of underendowed demon, what kind
of magician did they people their heaven, if
they now declare that this heaven is empty? And
why are they still searching, under this empty
heaven, for a world that is rational and good?

After reading this, my friend began an endless search for the soliloquy of "Yosl Rakover of
Tarnopol" described in the essay, as if he were
seeking a vanished document that described a God
for adults: a "personal God against Whom one can
revolt, which is to say for Whom one can die."

But he couldn't find it anywhere, not in
French nor in German, nor in any other language,
until he finally unearthed it in the cellars of the Munich State Library in a German periodical from
1956, in a yellowed translation. "Only he who has
recognized the veiled face of God can demand that
it be unveiled," Lévinas had written. If that was
true, one such rare man was now sitting in front
of me.

He was remarkable, I had heard in the meantime, very idiosyncratic—"quicksilver, a man whose
life had taken many strange turns, a brilliant and
chaotic temperament." Other things he'd written

were "insignificant," but his *Yosl Rakover* was "one great throw of the dice, a kind of 'Marseillaise' " (as if two such texts could be written in one lifetime). I learned this from Anna Maria Jokl, a writer who had escaped to Israel, and who first translated Zvi Kolitz, paradoxically, in Berlin in 1954 with the help of the Yiddish scholar David Kohan, and only afterwards discovered the author himself.

Naturally the text was still an enormous presence for her when I first called her in Jerusalem in December 1992. In an old-fashioned Bohemian accent, she told me that she remembered all too well how intensively she had had to work back then just to shape it into something printable. "The text was so terribly baroque!" Yes, where it was disturbing and sentimental and baroque she had had to "edit it into its final form," she also told me in her first letter. We talked for almost three-quarters of an hour, in great detail, about every imaginable detail of the contradictory story of how the piece had first been discovered. She was sure I could not imagine what she had put herself through in the service of this text. What she had endured was enormous. Yes, I was welcome to look over all the relevant documents in her apartment. The only thing she did not say a single word about was the fact that Zvi Kolitz was still alive.

She mentions this only weeks later, when I inform her of my upcoming trip to New York. Oh, hadn't she told me? No? How odd. Yes, of course he's alive, I now learn. He is "well settled and established, so to speak," and his "worldly habits" are, alas, the reason why he has long since "lost touch with the source of his own creativity." In advance of any new publication, therefore, it is essential that I allow her to explain things to me again—in detail, in Jerusalem. Otherwise she will not be able to grant me permission to reprint her *Yosl Rakover*. It is too important! So much depends on it. "Be careful!" she warns. "This story is full of traps. Can you imagine the attacks back then? He was savagely attacked. But I always interposed myself! So, please—no new mystifications!" Should I give Mr. Kolitz her greetings when I visit him? Greetings? No, no, that will not be necessary. "What a pity."—"Oh, you know, when it's over, it's over." Clearly, some deep quarrel lies beneath the old lady's connection to Mr. Kolitz these days and—"And don't think," her distant voice interrupts my thoughts, "that this is some love story

x

gone bad. No, no, it was much more serious than that! Much more serious!" She coughs. Her voice is creaking like an old door.

"Where did you get what you wrote about?" she asked Mr. Kolitz in 1955 in her first letter. "Who *are* you? I want the truth, are you a freak or a genius?" At that point she had already translated the text—though, admittedly, not as "a story by Zvi Kolitz" (about whose authorship she knew nothing at the time she was doing it) but as "The Testament of One Yosl Rakover from the Warsaw Ghetto."

"Who *am* I?" He replied, by return mail, "I am a Jew without any inferiority complex, and I believe in God"—although he would say things to God, if he ever met Him, that would make His hair stand on end. But the answer to where he got what he wrote must still begin with his birth.

Zvi Kolitz was born on December 14, 1919, between Grodno and Kaunas in Lithuania, in Alytus, a little town on the banks of the Nemen. "Six thousand Jews lived there, and not one of them was illiterate," he recalled. "I can still hear their singing in my ears—when they sang the psalms on the Sabbath. We lived in a wooden house right next to the synagogue, an enormous building made of red brick."

Zvi Kolitz is thus a Lithuanian Jew, a "Litvak." And Jewish Lithuania before the war was a whole world unto itself. "Lithuania," he observed decades later of his first homeland, "Lithuania was not a state but a state of mind." Truly, this country was unique on the map of Europe.

For seven hundred years, in contrast to all its neighbors, Jews had lived in Lithuania without a single pogrom. It was such a protected environment that it gave birth to its own ethnic sub-group, one that ranked as the intellectual and spiritual aristocracy of East European Jewry. The map of Lithuania was like a starry sky strewn with flourishing Jewish communities. In the towns, they made up approximately one-third of the population.

It was in Lithuania, in the eighteenth century, that Elijah ben Solomon Zalman totally resisted the magnetic influence of the Hasidic movement. For this the great opponent of irrationalism was lauded throughout the Jewish world as a genius, as the "Gaon of Vilna." His opinion, which held that the Jewish soul, with its tradition of the highest erudition, must open itself to the modern culture of the Christian world, became the basis of a specifically Lithuanian mentality, in which the house of study was more important than the house of worship, and the alphabet holier than prayer. The Jewish Enlightenment, which had begun in Germany, and which estranged untold numbers of Jews from the faith of their mothers and fathers— from Warsaw to London—strengthened Jewish culture in Lithuania in unprecedented fashion. In Lithuania there was, practically speaking, not a single uneducated Jew. In no other place in the world were there so many Yiddish newspapers, periodicals, publishing houses, and schools. Homer, Dante, Shakespeare, Goethe, Pushkin, Hegel, Dostoyevsky, Kafka, Chekov, Nietzsche, all the classic authors of world literature could be read and studied in Lithuania in Yiddish: all of modern culture.

In little Lithuania the Jewish calendar was almost more important than any other chronology (more even than in Israel, later). Until today, Zvi Kolitz knows the date of his father's death only as the twenty-second day of Tevet—a day that falls somewhere in January—and to this day he has no interest in placing it according to the Gregorian calendar. Nowhere else were Jews so unassimilated and so rich in political and cultural institutions. Nowhere else did Zionism also have such strong and deep roots.

This was the world in which Zvi grew up at

the feet of his father Nachmann, a highly regarded
rabbi and Talmudic scholar. His daring one-on-one
with God was something he first learned in the
schools of Alytus; Kierkegaard, it seems, had also
been translated from Danish into Yiddish in Lithuania. It was no accident that Emmanuel Lévinas
would later recognize the unknown author of *Yosl
Rakover* as an intellectual brother. For Lévinas, too,
was a Litvak—just like Monsieur Chouchani, his
secretive teacher, who surfaced as a "Mozart of the
Torah" in Paris after the war, before all trace of him
finally vanished in Montevideo.

Nachmann Kolitz died of diabetes at the age
of forty-four in 1930, when Zvi was not yet eleven
years old. "Never underestimate my love" were his
last words to his family, his neighbors, and the
members of the congregation who had crowded
into the dying man's room. Thus did the man stamp
the unformed boy at his feet like a coin. "He was
a prince of a man" is how Zvi Kolitz describes him
today, when he is more than thirty years older than
his father was back then. "I had a happy child-
hood," he told me the first time I met him, and then
his memory moved on to his mother, Hannah, who
had been born a Hesslson, a family from Eydtkuh-
nen, on the border between Prussia and Lithuania.

Though the family spoke only Yiddish and Hebrew at home, his mother also taught her favorite German poems to all of her children. German poems still come to his mind unbidden today, the memory of them not poisoned by his subsequent feelings about that language.

His last memory of Lithuania, where more than 160,000 Jews lived before the war, is the memory of the infernal eruption of anti-Semitism that suddenly ended the seven hundred years of respectful coexistence. This was why his mother left Lithuania with her four sons and four daughters—Louis, Zvi, Chaim, Itzhak, Malka, Rachel, Paya, and Rebecca—before Lithuania could be crushed between the millstones of Stalin and Hitler. Zvi was seventeen, a young Jew hungry for education, when he crossed a Germany gone mad on his way to Florence. He would exchange the endless bright summer evenings and long winter nights of his Baltic homeland for the sudden nightfall of the Mediterranean for almost twenty years. He would never return to Lithuania. The passionate traveler would never again see, or want to see, the pine woods of his home, the gentle lines of the hills, the quiet ponds.

He interrupted his exodus in Munich, where

he took advantage of a stop of the train to make an unauthorized tour of the area around the station and was shocked by the troubling calm in the capital of Nazism. Days later he said farewell to his family at the harbor in Trieste as they sailed for Palestine. He himself didn't follow them until after the outbreak of war, traveling then by way of Venice and Alexandria. It was Italy that had held him back, and fascinated him. In the meantime, with the Hitler-Stalin Pact, the Red Army rolled into Lithuania, where the dictators from the East immediately closed the Jewish schools, banned all Zionist organizations, arrested many intellectuals, and expropriated businesses and factories.

Zvi Kolitz reached Jerusalem in 1940, just as he turned twenty-one. The day he arrived was the last day in his life as a student of history in Florence. From now on he made history himself. He immediately joined Jabotinsky's movement, which was uncompromising in its efforts to create a Jewish state, *and* the Irgun, the radical group of underground conspirators who wanted to bomb the British out of the country. Yes, he was an extremist. From his days in Lithuania he was a passionate anti-Communist. He had no difficulty in recognizing the Leninist doctrine of human welfare as messianism run mad. His father had already impressed this upon him, and he had read Dostoyevsky's warning that "without God, anything is possible." But when, in the face of the worldwide Nazi threat that was bearing down on them, Kolitz still would not be silent about the horrors of Stalin and offered passionate testimony about the murderous dangers posed by messianic atheism, the young man was ridiculed, almost as if he were one of Dostoyevsky's own unworldly characters, a sort of Lithuanian Prince Myshkin—an "Idiot."

It was during this time that as a member of the Irgun he disappeared twice into British prisons—although his oldest brother, Louis, had given his life for England, dying in the fight against Hitler in July 1941 as a captain of the Royal Air Force during an attack on the battleship *Scharnhorst*. And today he himself sits in his armchair with the air of a retired British colonel, stroking a thin halo of hair back from his temples now and then with the palms of his hands, seductive, courteous, a gentleman. "The fight against the Empire was hard. But the English were still gentlemen in my eyes, even when I was sitting in their prisons." In present-day Israel, however, he is still haunted by some of his earlier exploits.

In June of 1941, while he was still exploring Palestine, German troops marched into Lithuania, where they were received by the inhabitants with bouquets of flowers. The Germans had broken the yoke of Bolshevism! But what Stalin had begun, Hitler now completed. Lithuania became part of the Reich's Eastern territory, and Lithuania sweated blood, but it was the blood of the Jews. The government of occupation began the persecution immediately, in preindustrial fashion—by hand, so to speak—with mass shootings that nonetheless remained eerily secret. News of the genocide could find virtually no way out to the wider world. On December 1, 1941, SS–Lieutenant Colonel Karl Jäger sent a nine-page letter, marked "Confidential: Affair of State," from Kaunas to Berlin, in which he gave an accounting, down to the minutest detail (with running totals carried over from page to page) of 137,346 people shot, and summarized as follows: "Today I can certify, that our goal of solving the Jewish problem in Lithuania has been accomplished by EK3 [*Einsatzkommando* 3]. Lithuania is free of Jews."

Zvi Kolitz remembers with perfect clarity the time when Rommel was pushing forward across North Africa toward Palestine, and Radio Crete was announcing hourly that the swastika flag would soon be fluttering from the Tower of David in Jerusalem. In the King David Hotel, meanwhile, the doorknobs were turned by kings and queens from all parts of the world. "The city had become a refuge of kings—yet at the same time we were working out plans to retreat, when the Wehrmacht attacked, into the caves around the Dead Sea. That was also when the Polish general Anders arrived from Siberia and brought Mr. Begin, who became the commander of the Irgun."

In 1942, for tactical reasons, the members of the Jabotinsky movement joined the British army, to concentrate all forces against the Nazis. Early the following year, in distant Warsaw, the Jews rose up, weapon in hand, against their overpowering oppressors, as the remaining population of the ghetto was about to be transported to the death camp of Treblinka. At the start of the Feast of Passover, the SS forced their way into the encircled ghetto with flamethrowers. Yet twenty-two groups of fighters suddenly opposed the SS units, and a thousand underground bunkers were already prepared for the resistance—the first comprehensively organized Jewish resistance since Roman times. For the first time since the rebellion of Bar Kochba, the "son of the stars" whom Rabbi Akiba had recognized as the Messiah, the Jews were rising in rebellion. Following the suppression of the revolt in the year 135, the emperor Hadrian ordered Rabbi Akiba to be flayed alive, and for the first time in world history an entire city was declared "purified of Jews." No circumcised male was permitted to enter Zion again. Now this fate was being repeated in the capital of Poland. "There is no more Jewish Warsaw" was SS–Brigadier General Jürgen Stroop's report to Berlin on May 16, 1943.

It was during these days that Zvi Kolitz was wearing the uniform of a Chief Recruiting Officer in Jerusalem. His enlistment coincided with his release from a British prison, and he spent the rest of the war traveling to Cairo, around Palestine, and throughout the entire Near East, recruiting as many Jews as possible as soldiers for the British army. He was also already working as a journalist, writing for the daily paper *Haboker* and weekly magazines. In addition, he had published a book of short stories in Hebrew, "a naïve book about events in Europe. In Israel we knew nothing until 1943." From then on, however, rumors flew around the country like swarms of black ravens. Rumors of mass murders in Poland. Rumors that the leaders of the Jewish Agency were suppressing the truth in order not to undermine the war effort—the blackest of rumors, innumerable rumors, and they increased from year to year. "Vilna drowned in Jewish blood," wrote the librarian Hermann Kruk, as he chronicled this period in Zvi's homeland, before he himself ended up on one of those enormous mounds of corpses that the victims themselves had to stack before they lay down on them and were shot in their turn. The mounds of corpses were still smoking when the Red Army reconquered Lithuania. Soviet soldiers photographed them. That was what the end of the unique Jewish community of Lithuania looked like. Only a fraction of the Jews had been able to escape, most often to the groups of Jewish partisans who had taken up the fight against the German Reich in the forests; one such group operated under the name Nekome, the Hebrew word for vengeance.

One last time, the little region of Lithuania outshone all other areas of the Jewish world in the force of its annihilation. Nowhere in the entire area of the world under Nazi domination were the Jews wiped out so radically as in the land where their culture had flourished with such a determination of its own. Only six percent survived the Shoah.

Only much later did Zvi Kolitz learn that his native community had been utterly destroyed by fire. "The entire congregation of Alytus was massacred—not by the Germans, no, by their Lithuanian neighbors. Not even the German soldiers could really believe that they could be so inhuman. They couldn't believe it. I knew every face." Nor to this day has he forgotten the faces of the murderers, who had lived next door to him as his neighbors.

Since that time, the old Lithuania truly exists only as a state of mind. Before I finished writing this account (in 1996), I went to see it for myself. I went, in particular, to the place that Zvi Kolitz wants never to see again. The former synagogue in Alytus, with its red and yellow bricks, had already long been a storehouse for salt; now it was a ruin, the doors nailed shut, the giant interior a wreck, the floor torn up, a refuge for wild animals. I put a small fragment of stone in my coat pocket. This is the "Beth Midrash," the shul of the old Jewish congregation, it says on a small plaque outside the door. I asked Jadviya Rimikieni, the daughter of the former baker, a woman with friendly bright eyes, to show me the house where Zvi had been born. "That's it," she said, standing in front of an imposing timbered building in Uzuolankos Street, literally next to the entrance of the synagogue. "This is where the handsome rabbi with all the children lived, the one who died so young." Six unemployed drunks now live in his family's house, which hasn't had a lick of fresh paint in decades. This Jewish street has become a street of the destitute.

Mrs. Rimikieni still knows one or two Yiddish songs that she learned from the children next door as a young girl. No, she confirms, there isn't a single Jew in Alytus any more. "The slaughter was terrible." The long-buried memory almost makes her ill, the memory buried under the memories of the forty-year Soviet rule that followed. Why it ever came to that, she never knew. It was not a question to be asked here. Now the lilac is in bloom, hens are cackling, a dusty road leads up the hill. The cantor lived just over there, and here to the right, the *shoykhet;* behind the house there's still the shed where he killed the hens.

Out in the forest we find mass grave after mass grave, and a small memorial marker that asks for "silence and reflection" because "the ground here is saturated with blood." In the war, Alytus became one of the biggest slaughter pits in the country; after those murdered from the town, another sixty thousand people from other occupied territories were hauled here and killed. Who in Germany has ever heard the name of this little place?

The old Jewish cemetery on the other side of the Nemen, by contrast, looks almost peaceful. The ancient gravestones rest in the grass of a little sun-filtered wood like the last glacial deposits from another era in earth's history. The sunlight flickers through its branches. Many gravestones have disappeared or been overturned and smashed, many graves broken open. After the last rain, the ground is scattered with flowers. The air smells of mushrooms. The Jews always throw small pebbles or grass over their shoulders as they leave the graveyard, the elderly baker's daughter had told us in the town. I pull up a small flower before we leave. Where is the grave of Nachmann Kolitz? A hole gapes in the decayed remains of an old rabbi's grave as if in a shattered skull.

In it lies rubbish, stones, shards, a small bottle, nothing more. The sign on the gate that identifies this place (in Yiddish) as "The Jewish Cemetery of Alytus," adds: "Blessed is the memory of the dead."

"In Palestine in 1943 we knew that something had been set in motion," Zvi Kolitz told me at our first meeting. "In 1944 we knew it for sure, but we had no idea of the extent." He fell silent. "I still remember," he then continued, shaking his head, "how we once discussed at a meeting what part of these rumors might be true. Some people stood up and said it was impossible. And then a man, Itzhak Grienbaum, a former member of the Polish parliament, leapt to his feet, banged his fists on the table, and yelled, 'They're annihilating us in Poland!' I don't know why we didn't believe him. Because he was a leftist? Because he was an atheist? I don't know. I didn't hear the words *gas chamber* until 1945."

After the war Zvi Kolitz found himself back in a British prison briefly, but soon he was traveling again, almost always with two sets of instructions: one official mission and one secret. Officially he was representing Jabotinsky's movement; unofficially he was representing the Irgun. He was also an expert in recruiting and enlisting, more active than ever, this time for a state not yet born. In 1946, at the age of twenty-six, he was the emissary of the Zionist World Congress in Basel, and shortly after that in Buenos Aires. A British military aircraft flew him on a mammoth and adventurous trip via Khartoum to the river Plate. Buenos Aires was also buzzing with rumors at that time. Only a year before, Argentina had declared war on Germany and immediately won. Now, in addition to the significant Jewish community, growing numbers of escaped Nazis were streaming into the German colonies there night after night. A fleeing SS officer from Solingen came ashore in the harbor unnoticed: Ricardo Clement, alias Adolf Eichmann, "the man who solved the Jewish question." Perón became dictator.

"The Argentinean Jews were also just in the process of discovering what had happened in Europe. I spoke every night about what we could do: that the only redress was the creation of a Jewish state." He clears his throat. "In Buenos Aires alone there were more than eighty thousand Jews. And between two speeches I had to give, I still remember it exactly, a man came to see me, a Señor Mordechai Stoliar, the editor of a local Jewish newspaper, and he asked if I would like to write something for their Yom Kippur edition. It was called *Di Yiddishe Tsaytung.* Sounds almost German, doesn't it! I told him, 'Yes, I have something in my head that I've wanted to unload for some time.' "

Shortly before this, the notes of Emmanuel Ringelblum had been found in Warsaw, buried in bottles and milk cans. His chronicle of the ghetto in December 1942 ended with the words: "Our subjugation has led to nothing. Never must something like this be permitted to happen again." And in a French special concentration camp in Vittel, between October 1943 and January 1944, the poet Itzhak Katzenelson wrote the long "Song of the Murdered Jewish People" and hid it in three bottles and buried them. These texts came to light quite soon after the war.

It is likely that even today a disproportionate number of texts, a true library of the Holocaust, lies scattered and moldering in the earth of Eastern Europe—most of them written in Yiddish. Not until 1978 were the buried bottles found in Radom in which Simcha Guterman had hidden his report, written on tiny strips of paper, of the expulsion of the Jews from Plozk. The doctor Lazair Epstein, the librarian Hermann Kruk, the poet Abraham Sutzkever had recorded the life and death of the Jewish community in Vilna and hidden it. The philosopher Benzion Rapaport concealed his last manuscript in a preserving jar, in which it outlived horror, fire, and destruction intact. Names link together with names to form rows in this tradition, in which leaving a record was understood as the last act of resistance, directed, above all, to those who would come after, and everything written down must be saved whenever possible, in bottles, cans, iron boxes—the way they had been two thousand years before in the clay jars that would be discovered in the caves of Qumran by the Dead Sea.

Since ancient times, rabbinical law has decreed that even the smallest shred of parchment or papyrus inscribed with all or part of the name of God must be protected from desecration. In our century this law concerning the *sheymes,* which is to say the "names," was widened by poets and writers in the pogroms of the First World War to cover all Jewish texts of witness: they must all be preserved and protected. It was a commandment. In the time of destruction, the name of Israel became as holy as the name of its God.

So Zvi Kolitz, too, sat down, sixteen months after the end of the war, as if he were the last of the chroniclers, belated and cut off from the others, to compose one last letter in a bottle documenting past events. He had witnessed nothing of what he was now going to commit to paper. But two decisive elements nonetheless made his testimony truer in a certain way than any eyewitness report.

First: though he had witnessed nothing, he *knew* more than any of the fighters in the ghetto the true extent of the Holocaust.

The second difference, however, is even more significant. Like the authentic witnesses to the catastrophe, Zvi Kolitz in his imaginary letter in a bottle also addressed himself primarily to the survivors and to the next generation. But then he suddenly, and radically, altered the recipient of his indictment. That same evening in his hotel room he began to write, and what he wrote was *Yosl Rakover Talks to God*.

"I was alone. It was in the City Hotel in Buenos Aires, and I still remember that the first thing that came to me was the ending. Then I had to think about the rest of it, between all the many speeches that I had to give every evening. But I still remember that I wrote the ending first, and the beginning last. It took me several days to lead the story back to its ending—a whole lifetime." He pauses again. "It was before there was a State of Israel."

Thus what we are also seeing here is the

young agent of the Irgun carrying over into his writing the unprecedented historical tension between the Warsaw Ghetto Uprising and the founding of the State of Israel. For the real experiences that nourished his account have their roots not in the destruction of the ghetto but in the Jews' fight for a protected new-ancient homeland in Palestine. The death struggle depicted in the story is thus in reality the initial labor pains of a unique and staggering birth. Already in Warsaw in 1943 a blue and white flag with the Star of David was raised in the battle for Muranovski Square, at the very heart of the horror. No spot was more bitterly defended. Before its founding, Israel had already risen up in Europe—against Germany. In Warsaw, the House of Jacob was no longer on its knees.

"Time and again, I remember, my father used to tell us that the entire history of Israel is reflected in the story of Jacob on the Jabbok—prefigured, yes! Jacob was alone. And someone wrestled with him until the first light of day, until he said to him, 'Let me go! You shall no longer be called Jacob but Israel, for you have wrestled with God and won.' This struggle, I felt, reached a new climax in the Warsaw Ghetto. Jacob knew he had no chance. Why did he wrestle with Him despite this? It was absurd." He stands up, folds his arms, and turns away. Whether he was paid for *Yosl Rakover* back then in dollars or in Argentinean pesos, and how much he was paid, he no longer remembers. The story appeared on September 25, 1946, for Yom Kippur—"Specially for *Di Yiddishe Tsaytung*, by Zvi Kolitz," as the headline stated. Some days later, on October 16, far away in Nuremberg, ten Nazi war criminals were hanged.

Does he still have the newspaper from Buenos Aires? "Of course, I must still have it here somewhere. I'll give it to you when you go." And what happened after that? "Well, the response was moving, and I thought: That's it. A year later the story appeared again in New York, translated into English, in a collection that was soon out of print, and that was the end of that."

That was absolutely not the end of that. It is true, however, that his life since then can be told in two different threads: one of personal biography, and the other of the career of *Yosl Rakover*—the "story of a story," a little detective piece. Because just like a message in a bottle, the text goes on its way across the oceans of the world. And unlike, indeed in exact reversal of, Pirandello's play about six characters in search of an author, soon after this story starts, it seems to be trying to shake off its author. Paradoxically, Kolitz's life since then can almost be sketched out more easily than the life of his fiction—although he himself has led several different lives: as a journalist, writer, propagandist, public speaker, filmmaker, businessman, theatrical producer, teacher, university lecturer, and gifted fund-raiser for the cause of Israel.

His biggest success is a film, *Hill 24 Does Not Answer.* It is the first film of the young State of Israel to win prizes at international film festivals at Cannes and in Mexico. I count six books in his bookcase that he wrote after that; among them: *Tiger Beneath the Skin* (a collection of short stories); *Survival for What?; The Teacher,* or *Confrontation.* All are out of print. He is currently at work on a new book, which is to be called *Genesis Revisited: Who Didn't Write the Bible?* In years past he produced attention-grabbing plays and musicals and suffered equally spectacular disaster (on Broadway). He still writes a regular column for *Der Algemeiner Journal,* a Yiddish newspaper in New York, and for *The Jewish Week.* Every Wednesday he lectures at Yeshiva University.

When Kolitz tells a story, Torquemada, the Grand Inquisitor, is as alive for him as the village priest of Alytus, or his father, or the Maharal of Prague. He sits amongst the hooting audience in the court of the king of Aragon as Nachmanides debates Pablo Christiani, the most famous converso of his time. The old rabbis and English poets people the world of his stories along with Ben Gurion and Martin Buber and the writer Else Lasker-Schüler, whom he met on his travels, either in Zurich or on the streets of Jerusalem.

When he met his second wife, Mathilde, in Mexico in the late forties, it was Yosl Rakover who brought about their marriage. The Sephardic beauty from an old family from Salonika copied down the text in one night from the first English translation, because she didn't know if she would ever see him again. There were no Xerox machines then. "I wrote all night," she recalls. For many years after that they lived only in hotel rooms—in New York or wherever in the world, later with their son Jonathan—and their only fixed address was an apartment in Tel Aviv. It was an existence on permanent call, an artist's or nomad's life.

But finally they settled in New York, where for so long they had always lived in hotels. Their apartment on the Mediterranean did not become their home, but even today memories creep out for him from under every stone in Israel, their annual trip to Jerusalem a single sigh. These days, this radical fighter for a Jewish homeland longs with all his heart only for peace for his country: peace with itself and peace with all its neighbors. He has been following the so-called peace process for years with bated breath. Every setback makes him sick. "If we'd stayed in Israel," says his wife, "Zvi would probably have been dead years ago."

"Nothing is as seductive as success," he says of his early departure to America. "Back then the success of my film lured me out of Israel." That he had had a falling out with Menachem Begin, until then his close friend, is another version I'd heard of why he left. "No," said his wife the first time we were alone, "I think he left Israel because of me, because I didn't speak Hebrew very well."

Who knows? As he explores the United States, he suddenly and unexpectedly crosses the thread of Yosl Rakover's life again. In the process of presenting his film in New York, he runs across a piece by the poet Jacob Glatstein in the Yiddish press about the lively discussion in Israel as to whether Yosl Rakover's speech to God is an authen-

tic document from the Warsaw Ghetto or a work of
the imagination, whether the author is still alive or
has already died.

"I didn't understand any of it. I had been
spending a lot of time with Ben Gurion in the desert
and reading nothing but the Hebrew press." He
laughs for a moment. "So I called up the newspaper,
and I wrote them a letter saying, 'I don't understand
this.' After all, I had never disowned my own
name."

But after all these years, Yosl Rakover had
taken on a life of his own—after first discarding the
name of his author. Just as Rabbi Löw had once
formed the Golem out of clay in the attic of the Alt-
neu Shul of Prague, so apparently had Zvi Kolitz
created "Yosl, son of David Rakover from Tarnopol" out of the letters of the Hebrew alphabet in
Buenos Aires. He had come to life. But Zvi Kolitz
had to pay for it with his own existence.

The following story can be reconstructed. In
1953 some unknown person in Argentina had sent a
typewritten "Testament from the Warsaw Ghetto"
to *Di Goldene Keyt* (The Golden Chain, a Yiddish
literary journal in Tel Aviv)—admittedly without
the headline, the name of the author, or the generic
label "Story." In the spring of 1954, the famous

Yiddish quarterly printed the text as "an authentic document." "The piece haunted us so much," Abraham Sutzkever, the publisher of the journal and legendary poet of the Vilna Ghetto, later acknowledged, "it seemed so genuine that we didn't think to ask any questions." Not only did Zvi Kolitz's correction come too late, it came as something unwelcome, and bore no fruit.

In January 1955 the "discovered document" is transmitted in a German radio broadcast by David Kohan and Anna Maria Jokl from the Free Berlin station. Two months later, still anonymous, it surfaces in a French translation of *La Terre Retrouvée*, a Zionist journal in Paris. The reverberations are uncanny. Thomas Mann reads the text and praises it, in a letter written shortly before his death, as a holy text, a "shattering human and religious document." Rudolf Krämer-Badoni writes a reply to Yosl Rakover, whose ashes he assumes are mixed in the ashes of Warsaw itself: "I have just read your letter.——How great must be your God, who can awaken such souls in mankind."

Even louder than these reverberations is the tumult of furious protest then unleashed by the letters of a certain Mr. Kolitz, writing not from the hereafter but from New York, in which he names himself as the author and makes clear that not only is he a living, mortal author but he was never in Warsaw. It's unforgivable! Anyone could claim the same thing. Why not say that Auschwitz was a figment of the imagination, too? And so on and so forth. Thus: *Fraud! Deceiver! Swindler! Scoundrel!* —and the text is suddenly seen in a completely new light. It does no good when Frau Jokl points out, "How do we know what the man looked like who wrote down the Book of Job?" The broadcast is repeated in October 1955 with the author's correct name; Frau Jokl writes an article in the *Tagesspiegel* and publishes her radio script the next year for the first time in the journal *Neuen Deutschen Heften* with a commentary. Yet eight years later, in 1963, in France, Emmanuel Lévinas publishes his wonderful essay on the discovered text by an "anonymous author" that is "as beautiful as it is real and true." The text is "so true," the philosopher immediately acknowledges, "as only fiction can be."

Two years later, in 1965, the text appears for the first time in a Hebrew translation in *Ani Ma'amin* in Jerusalem, where it is identified simply as a "testament." Again Zvi Kolitz points out the error, both amicably and in detail. Another three years later the text appears in an anthology in New York under his name, with a postscript explaining that although it is not an "authentic document," there had been a "Yosl Rakover, who died in the flames of Warsaw," whose fate had been known to the author. None of this is true. In the 1970s, a book appears in Israel reporting that *Yosl Rakover,* an anonymous document from the Warsaw Ghetto, has become the founding text of the radical settler movement Gush Emunim, and it is read again and again at meetings. In America it is inserted in prayer books, both Orthodox and Reform. "Friends who knew the story have told me," says Zvi Kolitz, "how on Yom Kippur in the great Conservative syna- gogue on Eighty-sixth Street, the rabbi introduced a famous actor who wished to read aloud a text from the Warsaw Ghetto. The pages had been found in the ruins after the suppression of the uprising. And he read *Yosl Rakover.* People wept. Afterwards my friends went to the rabbi and said, 'Rabbi, how can this be? We know the author.' And the rabbi said, 'I know there's an author. But this way it is much more moving.' That was perhaps five or six years ago. It's frightening. It distresses me, it makes me uneasy."

To multiply the contradictions, almost every text appeared in a slightly different form; each version differs more or less strongly from the others and all differ from the original. Just a few weeks ago he was asked to agree to a new translation from the Danish into Swedish. Because he has never read any new version thoroughly, even the translations he himself has paid for, there are always new speculations—and doubts—that start twining around his original authorship. His attitude has never been that of a literary man to the text he knows word for word—and this is unfathomable for critics.

A photo in a silver frame on a chest shows him in Mexico in the early '50s in a white linen suit like Carlos Gardel, the legendarily elegant "King of Tango": an unabashedly handsome young man, a ladies' man, or an adventurer. He may have been the one, he was certainly the other. The photo is from the days when he was getting to know his wife Mathilde. Even then he ate kosher, although he still smoked on the Sabbath; for the last thirty years he has not done that either on weekdays or on holy days. He never sets out on a journey without his prayer shawl; he begins every new day with a psalm.

Right to the end, he always spoke only Yid-

dish when he met with Isaac Bashevis Singer, who
for a long time lived a few blocks away. He has always read the *Jewish Daily Forward* for Singer's
stories, even if he disagrees profoundly with the
paper's leftist politics. He has never been comforted
by the appalling fashion in which history finally
confirmed his anti-Communist convictions, and the
past delivers up unimaginable mounds of corpses
of Bolshevist rule the way thawing snow reveals
what's underneath. Even in the eighties he was for-
bidden to set foot on Soviet soil on the specific or-
ders of the port authorities of Leningrad. The KGB
gave him more intense and uninterrupted scrutiny
than any literary critic—though not as much as he
got from Isaac Bashevis Singer, whose readings Zvi
Kolitz attended whenever possible. It was at a reading by Singer some years ago that he heard the
Nobel Prize–winner say in answer to a question
about his attitude to the Holocaust that he would
like to reply by referring to a story called "Yosl
Rekover ret tsu got." That was the way *he* thought
too. "He thought like Yosl. I couldn't believe my
ears. Like Jacob on the Jabbok."

But Jacob left that place both blessed and
wounded. So what was his blessing?

"You're asking what was my blessing? And

my wound? I will tell you what the blessing and the wound are. The wound *is* the blessing! I am a very happy man." He turns his head away and takes a deep breath through his nose. "I do not want to make any kind of a cult out of suffering. And yet happiness without suffering is a curse! Wait a moment." He gets up quickly and goes to his bookcase. "I have to read this to you, it's from Kazantzakis's *Journey to Sinai*." He puts on his glasses, leafs forward and backward. "Listen: 'Do you remember how Jehovah speaks to man?! How mountains and men crumble away in His hand, how kingdoms disappear beneath His foot? Man screams, howls, begs, crawls into caves, huddles in ditches—anything to escape Him. But Jehovah remains sunk in his heart like a dagger." He opens a thin hand. "This is the wound. The task we bear follows from this. It is the existential wound Heidegger speaks of, and it is more familiar to the Jews than to any other people in the world: the wound of life itself. I did not lose a single person in Auschwitz whom I knew, and yet not a day goes by when I am not moved to think about Auschwitz. I have become incapable of taking any tragedy *other* than personally, wherever it occurs. What happens in Bosnia affects me. What happens anywhere affects me. This is a wound. Pick up the newspaper—every day is a wound."

He suffers from depression, a deep melancholy that returns again and again. Obsessions large and small torment him, sleeplessness is no stranger. He calls it *"machalot nefesh*—it's what King David spoke of when he said, 'My soul is clouded within me.' " There is no medicine that is really effective against it. And yet he truly has a happy life and is full of humor, with an infectious laugh. He can beam like a boy. He has been a grandfather for years. Eight years before I met him, he lost his mother, then two sisters, Paya and Rebecca, and just recently, his brother Chaim. The lives of each of his brothers and sisters is its own novel. Except for his brother Louis, no one in his family suffered a violent death. He himself never killed anyone, nor was he in a position where he had to, despite all his war experience; in 1948 he was in the front lines in the siege of Jerusalem. Chaim wrote four books after retiring from a successful career in business; three were studies of great rabbis and one was a polemic against the unforgotten Yeschayahu Leibovitz, the great, pugnacious derider of Israel. Zvi's younger sister, Rachel, along with the sister of the above Professor Leibovitz, ranks among the greatest authorities in Israel on the Scriptures. Itzhak, his youngest brother, has been Chief Rabbi of Jerusalem since 1983.

A grandfather clock chiming every half-hour has given our conversation a regular beat, and eventually brings it to a close. His *Yosl Rakover* was a worldwide success, but without him; it did not make him world famous. "No," he says with self-assurance, "*Yosl Rakover* didn't change my life. He was my creation; he was formed by the convictions in which I grew up. How could the creation change the inner being of its creator?" It turns out he cannot find the original Argentinean edition that he wanted me to have. Please, will I excuse him? Unfortunately he's extremely disorganized and unmethodical. A pity.

Below the window dusk is settling over Central Park and the lights of the city are beginning to twinkle above the trees. A police siren dies away in the distance. I glance around the orderly apartment once more—the bookcases, the small marble table, the carpets, the paintings, the fireplace—while in compensation for the original he autographs a beautiful book to me with a couple of friendly lines. The book is the extremely painstaking work by a distinguished scholar from Chicago: an entire volume devoted exclusively to Yosl Rakover and that essay by Emmanuel Lévinas which first insightfully recognized the piece as fiction all those years ago and interpreted it like a modern psalm.

On the homeward journey I start to leaf through it a little and suddenly I sit bolt upright as I begin to read that this book employs a brilliant textual analysis to prove that the original was *not* written in Yiddish, but in English, and in New York. The book is, as the foreword accurately observes, "an intellectual feast." The Dutch author, a Professor van Beeck in Chicago, is a leading pupil of the German philosopher Gadamer. Is it possible that Zvi Kolitz hasn't ever read this book, either?

According to van Beeck's researches, an "anonymous translator" did a Yiddish version and offered it for publication in Tel Aviv. But that's not all. This translator also expanded the text in significant ways. The additions are identified and characterized word by word. I look at each one individually and see that together they represent all the high points of the colossal testament. The argumentation is fascinating.

Doesn't this make the whole thing even more of a beautiful riddle? Is it therefore—in almost biblical fashion—a textual magnet that has attracted new revisers all along the way, revisers who have perhaps contributed its best thoughts? But whatever the case: clearly, according to the thesis of this study, there is no Yiddish original from 1946. Why didn't Zvi Kolitz tell me this?

Professor van Beeck, whom I call immediately upon my return, is helpful to me in every way imaginable; never at any time when I have been doing research has such aid been lavished upon me. But this question is one he can't answer either. However, he immediately sends me an entire box full of his supporting evidence, among it English, French, and Spanish translations and, for the first time, the Yiddish text itself, from *Di Goldene Keyt* in Tel Aviv, and—even more important for me— a phonetic transliteration in Roman letters, which allows me to do my own translation.

In Buenos Aires, the telephone information service no longer has a listing for any "*Yiddishe Tsaytung,*" and the city is swarming with people named Stoliar whose fathers may once (perhaps) have published it. Jewish libraries from Berlin to New York cannot help, either, with a copy or a microfilm of the fateful broadsheet. On the offchance, I put in a call to the Jesuit College of Buenos

Aires. A Father Oscar Lateur answers. No, he can't help me. How could he? Besides, the good soul naturally has his own work to take care of. So what to do? My account of my meeting with Zvi Kolitz must be finished; my colleagues at the paper are already waiting for it. It is March 12, 1993. It will soon be the fiftieth anniversary of the uprising in the Warsaw Ghetto, when it is supposed to be published.

Discouraged, I open the newspaper and look at today's wounds: the rape of Bosnia, the shadows of the Horsemen of the Apocalypse approaching Russia, the death spiral of power in Palestine just before Passover. For several days now my brother Klaus has been in a hospital at the other end of town; he is dying. Every day I go over to see him, then back to my desk, where I work on a new translation from the Yiddish original into German. Then the fax machine rings, and the cylinder begins to hum. *B-u-e-n-o-s A-i-r-e-s* I read as the first page comes out of the machine. It is a chaotically pasted-together article in Hebrew letters, of which I understand not one stroke. Only the headline appears in the Latin alphabet. "EL DIARIO ISRAELITA— Miércoles 25 de Setiembre 1946." I am incapable of reading the text that follows and call up a friend who can decipher the Hebrew alphabet. The text must have yellowed terribly with age: it arrives so gray that you feel you can almost breathe the dust of the archives from which it must be coming. Huge inkblots decorate every sheet. The pages are blotchy, too pale here, too dark there, a piece missing in this place and that, and yet it is absolutely clear: "YOSL RAKOVERS VENDUNG TSU GOT"—and just below it, the word *Dertseylung* (story). And still further below, this: "*Spetsial far 'Di Yiddishe Tsaytung' fun* Zvi Kolitz." The next thing is an indecipherable introductory paragraph, and then, in clearer fragments: "*In eyner——shever Geto, tsvishn hoyens fun farsamelte shteyner un mentshliche beyner, iz gefunen gevorn——der folgender testament, geshriben fun a Yid . . .*" And further on, absolutely legible: "*Varshe, dem 28stn April 1943. Ich, Yosl der zun fun Dovid Rakover fun Tarnopol, a chossid fun Gerer Rebn un opshtamiger fun di tsadikim, gedolim un kedushim fun di mishpoches Rakover un Maysels, shrayb di dozige shures ven di heyzer fun Varshever Geto zenen in flamen . . .*"

It was enough. Father Lateur had searched for the text in a library in the Calle Pasteur, in the so-called Jewish Quarter of Buenos Aires, with the help of a "good Señora Elena," found it, and hastily made a copy in its several parts exactly as he found it, and faxed it to me in Germany.

A few days later I had finished my article; that same evening, my brother died. On Friday, April 23, 1993, the early version of the texts on Zvi Kolitz and Yosl Rakover appeared in the magazine supplement of the *Frankfurter Allgemeine Zeitung*.

In New York, Kolitz was happy that his authorship would finally be recognized once and for all. But not even forty days later, Chaim Be'er, the popular author, published an article in the newspaper *Ha'aretz*, saying that *Yosl Rakover Talks to God*, the most profound piece of writing brought forth by the Holocaust, was alas a forgery. And in Frankfurt, meanwhile, a letter from Frau Jokl in Jerusalem appeared among the Letters to the Editor protesting furiously and energetically my plagiarism and counterfeiting of her "original." Shortly afterwards a complete copy of the entire story arrived in the mail from Buenos Aires.

During this period an acquaintance also showed me a modern religious textbook for high school students, in which there were excerpts of the text, identified as a "Jewish confession by Yosl Rachover, showing the influence of the spirit of the Hasidim." So there it was, in a school reader that months ago I had been unable to find and had never seen—there it was, if only in excerpts, under an incorrect author's name, and followed by an "exercise": "Describe the belief that can be found in this text. Compare the text with Ivan Karamazov's protests to God. Is Yosl Rachover a modern Job?"

Just the other day, a "Prayer by Yosl Rakover that he wrote in the burning Warsaw Ghetto as part of his testament" also came to my attention. "Lord, I came into the world to believe in You. . . . You, however, have done everything to make me not believe in You. . . . You make me a scrap of meat thrown to mad dogs, You brand me with the mark of shame. . . ." And after Yitzhak Rabin's murder, "Yossele Rackover's Last Will and Testament" was also quoted in the *Jerusalem Post*—"found in the ruins of the Warsaw Ghetto." The myth persists, solid as a rock.

Meanwhile, documents and letters to, from, and about Zvi Kolitz have collected to fill six fat binders in my bookshelves. In America, Yosl Rakover's speech to God was published again last year, along with a new and very fine study by Professor van Beeck and other scholars. My piece for the magazine was reworked in the fall of 1994 and published as a small book. It didn't have the slightest

72

effect on the *Yosl Rakover* myth. Yosl Rakover travels according to his own laws, and his journey is still not over.

"*Yosl Rakover* is the story of a Jew possessed by his faith as if by a Dybbuk," Isaac Bashevis Singer said before he died. In the summer of 1994, I pulled together some similar quotes, which we wanted to use to help promote the little volume with its awkward title that was the first presentation of the whole story in book form. A letter from George Steiner stated that this figure was proof that the Jews suffered from "Godsickness"—just as others suffered from homesickness or lovesickness. In a commentary, the theologian Klaus Beger compared Yosl Rakover's lament not only with the books of Job and Ezra, but also with the ninth chapter of Paul's epistle to the little congregation in Rome.

Then, on the morning of July 18, I heard on the car radio that "a synagogue" in Buenos Aires had been blown up. Later news reports during the course of the day revealed that at 9:55 A.M. the building housing a Jewish-Argentinean aid organization, at number 633 Calle Pasteur, had been completely destroyed in a bomb attack. The timing of the attack had been deliberately chosen to ensure that the maximum number of employees would be in their offices, and almost two hundred people were in the seven-story building. The explosion could be heard all over the city. Hours later the narrow street in the Barrio del Once was still an inferno. Digging all the bodies out of the rubble—some killed in the blast, some buried alive, others severely injured—would take days.

It was the same house in which, a year before, Elena Berlfein and Father Lateur had rediscovered the original of Zvi Kolitz's story. The radio mentioned a library that had been on the third floor of the house. That's where the text must have been. I imagined that the archival volumes of *Di Yiddishe Tsaytung* had been covered in dust; the local paper had ceased publication many years before. How long had Elena Berlfein leafed through them? She had to check every page of every edition published in September 1946, for the supposed masterpiece she was searching for at Father Lateur's request was not listed on any contents page. She eventually found it, amid advertisements for a Polish bank, a tailor, a lighting fixtures shop, a shop selling spats, another selling ball bearings, and a bed manufacturer, way at the back of the last issue before Yom Kippur, on pages 39 and 40, as her finger ran along the line, "*In eyner fun di khurbones fun Varshever*

Geto . . . iz gefunen gevorn . . . der folgender testament. . . ."

I suddenly saw Zvi Kolitz in front of me again. "Do you know what tortures me most horribly? That up until now we still have not read anything that begins to put into words what really happened to us. We have no expression of the truth. It is a wound that cannot heal. Nobody can say it for us. We are not in a position to have it. It cannot be expressed. And perhaps we may not and should not have it." But of course he doesn't stop going on searching for words, his own and other people's. "The Holocaust is a kind of hole in the cosmos"— this is something he had read recently, he wrote me in a recent letter. "It is a guarantee of the existence of evil. For the Jews, it is now an answer to the crucifixion."

That evening I brought down a carton from the bookcase and took another look at the blotched copies that I had stuffed into it after Father Lateur had sent me a clearer set by mail. I had assembled them myself with scissors and glue. Still, it is marred by more than one typographical error, I have been informed, and the punctuation was rather slapdash. Two or three passages seem garbled. The typesetter in Buenos Aires hadn't paid much attention to what he was doing. Here and there the text makes sudden jumps of its own. The transitions are sometimes odd. Questionable logic and contradictions, things that didn't make sense, and repetitions don't seem to have bothered the author, nor were stylistic imperfections of any concern to him. Compared to this, the later "anonymous" version from Tel Aviv was really flawless. Under the editorial hand of the poet Abraham Sutzkever, the laconic text had become more elegant. Is this, perhaps, the final peculiarity of the original version? Everyone who has worked on it has always tried to improve it in his or her own way, myself included.

No matter. The copies came to me from Argentina just in time. This glued-together patchwork in the carton in front of me has thus become the new original. This paper jigsaw puzzle was now the thing itself and would carry the text into the next millennium—the "forgery" that would survive us all as one of the rare true documents of our time.

That same evening I called Zvi Kolitz, to whom every attack on the House of Jacob still comes as an attack on his own family, full of shock and pain, as if in old age he had to catch up on all the suffering that he escaped in Europe in his youth. We didn't talk for long. He had, of course, heard about the assault; he didn't know that it had destroyed the building in which his text had been rediscovered. I told him. He repeated it in disbelief. "Is it really true," he asked, "that the pages are now literally lying buried under a heap of charred stone and human bones?"

Loving the Torah More Than God
by Emmanuel Lévinas

Among the recent publications on Judaism
in the West are a number of beautiful texts. Talent
in Europe comes easy. True texts are rare. As Hebrew studies have dried up in the last hundred years,
we have been distanced from their wellsprings. The
knowledge that still emerges is not grounded in an
intellectual tradition. It is autodidactic, even when
not actually improvised. And to be read by no one
but those less knowledgeable than oneself is cor-
rupting to an author. Without critics or sanctions,
authors confuse this lack of resistance with liberty,
and this liberty with proof of genius. It is no sur-
prise that readers don't trust this and see in Judaism,
which still finds itself claimed by millions of those
who have fallen away from it, a mass of trivial and
worldly quibbles.

I have just read a text that is both beautiful and true, true as only fiction can be. Published in an Israeli literary journal by an anonymous author, translated for a Zionist magazine in Paris, *La Terre Retrouvée*, by Arnold Mandel, under the title of *Yosl, Son of David Rakover of Tarnopol, Talks to God*, it seems to have aroused emotion in its readers. It deserves more. It evinces an intellectual stance that reflects more than intellectuals' readings, more than concepts borrowed from Simone Weil, for example, the last word in religious terminology according to everyone in Paris. On the contrary, this text is the bearer of Jewish learning, discreetly hidden but unerring, and it expresses a profound and authentic experience of spiritual life.

The text presents itself as a document written during the last hours of fighting in the Warsaw Ghetto. The narrator has apparently witnessed all the horrors; he has lost his young children in horrific circumstances. The last surviving member of his family, but for only a brief interval, he leaves us his last thoughts. Literary fiction, to be sure; but fiction in which all of us who survive recognize ourselves with a sense of vertigo.

I am not going to tell the whole story, although the world has learned nothing and forgotten everything. I refuse to offer up the ultimate Passion as a spectacle and to use these inhuman screams to create a halo for myself as either author or director. The cries are inextinguishable; they echo and re-echo across eternity. What we must do is listen to the thought that they contain.

What is the meaning of the suffering of innocents? Does it not prove a world without God, an earth on which man is the only measure of good and evil? The simplest and most common reaction would be to decide for atheism. This would also be the reasonable reaction of all those whose idea of God until that point was of some kindergarten deity who distributed prizes, applied penalties, or forgave faults and in His goodness treated men as eternal children. But I have to ask these people: With what kind of underendowed demon, what kind of magician did they people their heaven, if they now declare that this heaven is empty? And why are they still searching, under this empty heaven, for a world that is rational and good?

Yosl, son of David, experienced the certainty of God's existence with new force in an empty world. Because if Yosl exists in his utter solitude, it is so that he can feel all of God's responsibilities resting on his shoulders. On the road that leads to the one God there is a way station where there is no God. Genuine monotheism owes it to itself to respond to the legitimate demands of atheism. A grown man's God shows Himself in the very emptiness of a childish heaven. In the moment when He withdraws from the world and veils His face, as Yosl says, "He has delivered mankind over to its own savage urges and instincts." And, "When the forces of evil dominate the world, it is, alas, completely natural that the first victims will be those who represent the holy and the pure."

The God Who veils His face is neither, I think, a theological abstraction nor a poetic image. It is the hour when the just individual can find no external reprieve, when there is no institution to protect him, when the consolation of a divine presence within childish religious feelings is also denied, when the individual can triumph only in his own conscience, which necessarily means through suffering. Suffering in its specific Jewish sense, which never takes on the value of a mystical expiation for the world's sins. The situation of the victims of a world in disorder, which means a world in which the good cannot triumph, is suffering. It reveals a God who renounces any manifestation of Himself that would give succor, and calls on man in his maturity to recognize his full responsibility. But this God, this distant God, Who veils His face and abandons the just man to a justice in which there is no victory, springs immediately from within. The man's consciousness experiences this intimacy as part of his pride in being a Jew, of belonging factually, historically, plain and simple, to the Jewish people. "To be a Jew is to be . . . an eternal swimmer against the roiling, evil current of humanity. . . . I am happy to belong to the unhappiest of all peoples in the world, whose Torah embodies the highest law and the most beautiful morality."

Intimacy with the powerful God is attained through an extreme ordeal. Because I am a member of the Jewish people in their suffering, the distant God becomes *my God*. "I know now that You are my God. For You are not, You cannot be the God of those whose deeds are the most horrific proof of their militant godlessness." The just man who suffers for a justice in which there is no victory is the living embodiment of Judaism. Israel—historical and physical—becomes once again a religious category.

The God Who veils His face and yet is recognized as being present and inside oneself—is this possible? Is this a metaphysical construct, a paradoxical *salto mortale* in the manner of Kierkegaard? I think, on the contrary, that this is a particular manifestation of the nature of Judaism: the connection between God and man is not a sentimental communion within the love of a God made flesh, but a relation of minds mediated by instruction, through the Torah. It is precisely the Word itself, not incarnate, that assures us of the living God among us. Belief in a God Who does not manifest Himself by any terrestrial authority can only be grounded in internal evidence and the value of an education. To the honor of Judaism, there is nothing blind in this belief. Which is what gives rise to Yosl's remarks that are the culminating moment of the soliloquy and carry within them the echo of the Talmud in its entirety: "I love Him. But I love His Torah more. Even if I were disappointed in Him, I would still cherish His Torah."

Blasphemy? At the very least, a protection against the madness that comes from direct contact with the Sacred without the mediating power of reason. But above all a trust, which does not rest on any victorious institution and which is the internal evidence of the morality given by the Torah. A hard journey both in spirit and in reality, and one that holds no mysteries. Simone Weil understood nothing about the Torah. "While our God is the God of vengeance," says Yosl, "and our Torah threatens death for the smallest of transgressions, it is also told in the Talmud how in ancient times, when the Sanhedrin was our people's highest court . . . a single death sentence from the High Council in seventy years was enough to make people call 'You murderers' after the judges. The God of other peoples, however, whom they call 'the God of Love,' has offered to love every creature created in His image, and yet they have been murdering us without pity in His name day in, day out, for almost two thousand years."

Man's true humanity and his powerful gentleness make their entrance into the world in the severe words of a demanding God; the spiritual does not impart itself in anything of substance; it is an absence. God manifests Himself not by incarnation but by absence. God manifests Himself not by incarnation but in the Law.

His grandeur is not contained in the breath of sacred mystery. His grandeur does not provoke fear and trembling, it fills us with the highest thoughts. His divine grandeur is shown when He veils His face in order to ask everything, to ask the superhuman, of man; it is shown in His creation of a man capable of responding, capable of approaching God as a creditor and not always as a debtor. The creditor has faith in abundance, but also does not resign himself to the evasions of the debtor. This soliloquy starts and finishes with this refusal of resignation. Capable of trusting an absent God, this man is also an adult who measures his own weakness: the heroic situation in which he finds himself makes the world precious, but it also puts him in danger. Matured by a faith that springs from the Torah, he reproaches God for His unbounded grandeur and His excessive demands. He will love Him in spite of all that God has attempted to turn away his love. But "You should not pull the rope too tight" is Yosl's cry. A religious life cannot be achieved in such heroic circumstances. God must reveal His face, justice and power must be reconnected, there must be just institutions on this earth. Only he who has recognized the veiled face of God can demand that it be unveiled. It is within this rigorous dialectic that God and this man's equality establishes itself at the very heart of the disproportion between them.

We are as far from the warm, almost palpable communion with the Divine as we are from the despairing pride of the atheist. This is humanism in all its integral austerity, bound to a demanding love. And, inversely, a love that coincides with a man's exaltation. A personal, unique God does not reveal Himself like an image in a darkened room. This text shows how ethics and the ordering of principles found a personal relationship worthy of the name. To love the Torah more even than God is to gain access to a personal God against Whom one can revolt, which is to say for Whom one can die.

A Privation of Providence
by Leon Wieseltier

In his commentary on *Yosl Rakover Talks to God*, Emmanuel Lévinas did not allow himself to be detained by the question of the text's authenticity, and he was right. The inauthenticity of Zvi Kolitz's story is the inauthenticity of art; and art was not retired even by the incalculable atrocity of 1939–1945. This inauthenticity is merely historical. Kolitz did not witness the extermination that his narrative describes, he imagined it, and—this especially infuriates his critics—in the first person; and for this reason some of his critics have accused him of forgery. But this is an error, an emotion. If Kolitz presumes to think and to feel like the final survivor in a room of corpses in the final hours of the Warsaw Ghetto, it is because such is the founding presumption of fiction. To seek the true it leaves the real. The temerity of *Yosl Rakover Talks to God* is the temerity of the imagination. And the imagination has always been an indispensable instrument for the consideration of tragedy, not least because its point of regard is not empirical.

But was this tragedy like any other tragedy, so that it may stimulate art like any other art? There are those who believe that it was not like any other tragedy; and in some respects it was not. The imagination of the Holocaust seems to offend against "the uniqueness of the Holocaust." In the case of this catastrophe, it seems, our duty is only to secure the facts and to bow before them. But the doctrine of "the uniqueness of the Holocaust" is an awful doctrine. As a proposition of history, certainly, "the uniqueness of the Holocaust" is specious. Who would deny that the fate of the Jews in Europe between 1939 and 1945 was, in certain essential ways, similar to the fate of the Jews in other European times and in other European places? The discontinuities must not obscure the continuities, or else the Jewish experience of European evil will not be grasped in its full scope and its full duration. Regarded in the light of the Jewish tradition's pessimism about the exile, the Holocaust is chillingly coherent. It was certainly not the first time that an attempt was made to destroy Judaism by destroying the Jews; by erasing them physically. The Holocaust was indeed "worse," but if it was worse, then it was not "unique."

The doctrine of "the uniqueness of the Holocaust" also has the consequence of ripping the disaster so far out of history that it becomes incommensurable, in the way that the sacred is incommensurable. But the Holocaust was the precise opposite of the sacred. It was profane, in both connotations of the word: obscene, and secular, or lived by its victims as their experience, without respite or rescue or revelation. The memory of their experience must not be abused, but it must not be made exceptional beyond all recognition, and thereby insulated against our need. The literary critics who patrol contemporary literature for imprecise Holocaust metaphors, the political critics who patrol contemporary politics for imprecise Holocaust analogies—they ought to be sometimes a little forgiving. An imprecise analogy is not a false analogy; and it may be a useful analogy, for moral thought and moral action. (When Elie Wiesel insisted in a refugee camp at the border of Kosovo that the fate of the Jews was different, his presence there suggested that it was also the same.) Before

Jews are Jews, they are human beings; and so the meaning of their history is never so unique that it is not also universal.

When Auschwitz is the object of one's mind, who is not in a situation of analytical desperation? We need all the help that we can get. Since we will never understand Auschwitz adequately, let us avail ourselves of all the faculties of the mind and the heart. Let us hear all the theories and all the stories, so that we may seize any ray that a theory or a story may throw. There will be theories and stories that are false and mean, but they will not make the darkness darker.

The mystification of the horror is a poor way to honor the magnitude of the horror. Those who sacralize the destruction impede the understanding more than those who imagine it; and so Zvi Kolitz's imposture of Yosl Rakover is a perfectly legitimate stab at sense. But its legitimacy tells nothing about its quality, and the artistic achievement of *Yosl Rakover Talks to God* is not very considerable. The story is, really, a shriek. It reads as if it was written by a fist. It introduces no complication into its character, preferring the easy eloquence of a perfect victimhood. There is altogether too much clarity. The narrator's description of himself as "an ordinary living man who had the great but terrible honor of being a Jew" is affecting, but it is immediately followed by the assertions that "I am proud to be a Jew," and that "I am proud of my Jewishness," and that "I believe that to be a Jew is to be a fighter," and that "being a Jew is an inborn virtue": slogans all, and the misplaced remnants of an ideological rhetoric. (These flat, fervent exclamations put me in mind of Dov Landau in *Exodus*.) Kolitz's slogans have the effect of stirring a sentiment of solidarity in the reader, which is precisely the wrong sentiment. It rescinds the shock. Solidarity, with this last man at this last moment? It is an effrontery. We are not Yosl Rakover's familiars.

But it is not Yosl Rakover's ideology that makes the text interesting. It is Yosl Rakover's religion. Lévinas was correct to kindle to the theological dimension of Kolitz's narrative. *Yosl Rakover Talks to God* is one of the earliest articulations of the concept that became a central feature of the postwar Jewish attempt to explain the recent hell: *hester panim*, or the "hiddenness of the Face."

In Judaism, the concealment of God from man has a metaphysical meaning and a historical meaning. It is a term of theosophy and a term of theodicy. Metaphysically considered, *hester panim* refers to the essential unknowability of God. For the philosophers, this was the problem of the otherness of the Divine, which mandated the reading of God's attributes as allegories; for the kabbalists, this was the problem of the infinity of the Divine, which came to be called the *Ein-Sof*, or "the Limitless." An early kabbalist defined God as "that which the mind does not reach." For both the philosophers and the kabbalists, the unreachability of God was the measure of man's finitude. Historically considered, however, the unreachable God was the consequence not of human finitude but of human turpitude. It was a punishment for sin.

This construction of the absence of God was introduced in the Bible, near the conclusion of Deuteronomy, in famously frightening words: "Then my anger shall be kindled against them in that day, and I will forsake them, and I will hide my face from them, and they shall be devoured. . . . And I will surely hide my face in that day for all the evils which they shall have wrought. . . ." The darkness in which men move is here a punitive darkness. Maimonides observed about these verses that "the signification of this is that the Divine Presence has

been removed. This removal is followed by a privation of providence, as far as we are concerned. As it
says by way of a threat, 'And I will hide my face
from them, and they shall be devoured.' " Yet this
removal is not a motion of cosmology. It is a motion
of morality. The presence of God is a reward, the
absence of God is a punishment. "It is clear that
we are the cause of this hiding of the Face," Maimonides continued, "and we are the agents who
produce this separation."

When Yosl Rakover adduces the notion of
hastoras ponim, he takes his place in an old tradition
of Jewish theodicy. And then he proceeds to undo
it, to twist it into the design of his desperation.
Theologically, the accomplishment of *Yosl Rakover
Talks to God* is to have stripped the hiddenness of
the Divine between 1939 and 1945 of its punitive dimension, so as to let it stand as an act of celestial
cruelty. "I do not say, like Job, that God should lay
His finger on my sins so that I may know that I have
earned this. For greater and better men than I are
convinced that this is no longer a question of punishment for sins and transgressions. On the contrary, something unique is happening in the world:
hastoras ponim—God has hidden His face." What
could the Jews have done to deserve what was done

to them? Nothing, plainly. Thus the absence of God is not an expression of justice. It is an expression of injustice. This is Kolitz's radicalism: he transforms the privation of providence from an effect into a cause. And by the standards of the traditional understanding of *hester panim*, this is indeed "something unique." Spiritually, the dissociation of suffering from sin clears the ground for the believer's rage. It makes Yosl Rakover's anger almost into an analysis.

Kolitz's tale does not tamper with the believer's cosmos. It owes its power in part to its philosophical conservatism. There is God, and there is man, and they are not to be mistaken for each other. The structure is bitter, but it is intact. Yet Lévinas's reading of Kolitz's tale disrupts the structure. He turns an absence into a presence; and in so doing he robs Yosl Rakover's libel of its metaphysical tension, by diminishing it into an ethical tension. This is in keeping with Lévinas's religion of immanence, with his lifelong enterprise of conferring upon morality the glamour of transcendence.

Ce Dieu lointain vient du dedans, Lévinas writes in the climactic sentence of his commentary. This distant God comes from within—that is, from the voice of conscience. This God "calls on man in

his maturity to recognize his full responsibility";
and this is all that this God does, except to disappear. But surely a God that comes from within is not
a God that is distant. Surely such a God is near, very
near, so near that He may be said to be ourselves,
and merely the hallowed name of our highest stan-
dard. Lévinas thinks that he is deriving morality
from religion, but he is deriving religion from
morality. And with this lowering conception of the
deity, he parts company with the text that he ad-
mires. For the title of the text is *Yosl Rakover Talks
to God*, not *Yosl Rakover Talks to Yosl Rakover*.

Lévinas's commentary was given as a radio
talk in 1955, and it is a document of its day. When he
writes of "the refusal of resignation" in Yosl Rakover's narrative, and of the "heroic situation" that
"makes the world precious, but also puts him in
danger," Lévinas has enrolled Yosl Rakover in the
ranks of what used to be called religious existentialism. "We are as far from the warm, almost palpable
communion with the Divine as we are from the
despairing pride of the atheist," he concludes with
satisfaction. "This is humanism. . . ." But humanism
does not require the Torah. Indeed, humanism's
alienation from religion was a condition of its de-
velopment. For humanism, Kant will do just fine,

and so will Marcus Aurelius. Nor is Lévinas quite so equidistant between the mystic and the atheist. He is much closer to the atheist, because his religion of ethics can find a place in the atheist's universe but not in the mystic's universe. In the mystic's universe, the revelation is not human.

Lévinas wants the courage of the atheist and the certainty of the theist. I do not see how he can have both, in his reflection on Yosl Rakover and in his other writings. The problem will not go away by declaring romantically that "God manifests Himself not by incarnation but by absence" and taking pleasure in the paradox. For this is not a paradox, it is a contradiction. The idea of a God who manifests Himself by not manifesting Himself is an idea in need of an explanation. Until then, it is only an intellectual's incredibility. Until then, an absent God is a God who has *not* manifested Himself, and the rest is nothing more than desire, which is an engine of superstition.

There are people, moreover, for whom even the absence of God is absent, who are shaken not by the privation of providence but by the privation of the privation, who live in a completely ungoverned and unconsoling world. To use the terms of another religious existentialist of Judaism against him: there is a man who is lonelier than the lonely man of faith, and he is the lonely man of no faith. There is solitariness! Religious existentialism was always a little complacent. It was never as heroic as it believed. An absconded God is not a variety of skepticism, it is a variety of enchantment—a discrete and convenient enchantment that found favor in modernity, because it spares God and man the embarrassments of each other's company.

The unhappiness of an individual who believes that there is a God cannot decently be compared to the unhappiness of an individual who does not believe that there is a God. But there was a being to whom Yosl Rakover could make his address. In this sense, and only in this sense, it may be said that Yosl Rakover was lucky.

About the Author

Zvi Kolitz was born in Lithuania in 1919, the son of a renowned rabbi. He arrived in 1940 in Palestine, where he joined the Jewish underground in their battle against the British Mandatory authorities to form the State of Israel. He then lived for several years in South America, eventually settling in New York City, where he has worked as a filmmaker, a Broadway producer, and a lecturer at Yeshiva University.

A Note About the Translator

Carol Brown Janeway's translations include
Binjamin Wilkomirski's *Fragments*, Marie de
Hennezel's *Intimate Death*, Bernhard Schlink's
The Reader, and Jan Philipp Reemtsma's *In the
Cellar*.